10.95

DATE DUE		
MAR 18 1990		
MAY 18 1991		
AUG 2 1991		
NOV 29 1991		
DEC 23 1991		
MAY 3 1992		
MAR 7 - 2002		

HIGH SMITH REORDER #45-230

FAMOUS

BUILDERS

OF CALIFORNIA

FAMOUS

BUILDERS

OF CALIFORNIA

E D W A R D   F.   D O L A N,   J R.

Illustrated with photographs and prints

DODD, MEAD & COMPANY · New York

PICTURE CREDITS
California Historical Society, San Francisco, 17, 22–23 (Challis Gore), 36 (Carleton E. Watkins), 45 (print from The National Archives), 53, 58–59 (McCurry), 90, 98–99, 110 (Hartsook), 115; Wells Fargo Archives, San Francisco, 70, 71, 75.

Distributed in Canada by
McClelland and Stewart Limited, Toronto
Manufactured in the United States of America

1 2 3 4 5 6 7 8 9 10

Library of Congress Cataloging-in-Publication Data

Dolan, Edward F., date
  Famous builders of California.

  Bibliography: p.
  Includes index.
  Summary: Traces the lives of seven individuals instrumental in shaping the history of California including Father Junipero Serra, John Sutter, and Luther Burbank.
    1. California—Biography—Juvenile literature.   2. Pioneers—California—Biography—Juvenile literature.   3. California—History—Juvenile literature.   [1. California—Biography.   2. California—History.   3. Pioneers]   I. Title.
CT225.D65   1987   979.4   [920]   87-587
ISBN 0-396-08847-3

FOR TIM, JEANIE,
BETSY, AND GRANT

CONTENTS

INTRODUCTION

The Fabulous Land

When the Spanish came to the New World and conquered Mexico in the early 1500s, they began to hear strange Indian legends. The legends spoke of a fabulous island far to the north. It was said to be inhabited by giants and rich in gold. In time, this island was found to be not an island at all. It turned out to be a great stretch of land on the west coast of the North American continent. It is today the state of California.

No one knows whether the tales were actual legends or whether the Indians of Mexico made them up in the hope that the Spanish invaders would go away in search of all that gold and leave them in peace. Whatever the case, the Spanish did indeed go looking for the fabulous land.

9

Several explorers tried to find it by hiking north from Mexico. They failed to reach their destination. But, along the way, they became the first outsiders to visit today's Texas and New Mexico.

Two sea expeditions did better. They reached the California coast in the early 1500s. Both sailed along much of its length before turning for home.

Because of those voyages, the Spanish claimed that the land of legend belonged to them. They held it as a possession until the Mexican people overthrew them and established Mexico as an independent nation in the 1820s. California then became a Mexican possession.

It remained as such until the United States won it in the Mexican War of 1846–48. Soon thereafter— on September 9, 1850—California was admitted to the Union as the thirty-first state.

California is today a land that many people think to be as fabulous as the old legends made it out to be. As the Indians of Mexico had said, it does contain some gold. But it is far richer in other ways— in its scenery, its oil resources, its many farm products, its industries, and its people of every nationality. It is home for more than 25,600,000 people. This makes it the most heavily populated of our states.

Many people have played a part in the history of California. Each helped to build it into the state that it is today. In this book, we're going to meet seven of those people. They all lived exciting lives. They all did especially important work for California. They can all be truly called famous builders of California.

CHAPTER ONE

Father Junipero Serra

IT was the morning of November 24, 1713. Antonio Serra looked down at his newborn son. The infant lay very still in his mother's arms. His face was deathly pale. The little one was just a few minutes old.

Antonio was sure that his son was going to die. He wrapped the tiny body in a blanket and ran out into the cold. His dash took him to the village priest. He wanted the boy to be baptized into the Catholic faith before death came.

But the child—Miguel José Serra—did not die. He lived to do important work in a land clear across the world from his home. He lived to build a series of churches, known as missions, throughout California.

AN ISLAND BOY

Miguel José was born and raised on the island of Majorca. Majorca lies in the Mediterranean Sea near Spain. The boy's parents were poor Spanish farmers. They made their living by working a few acres outside the fishing village of Petra.

Miguel's childhood was marked by many illnesses. Just as he had been at birth, he was frail as a boy. Time and again, he fell sick. His illnesses kept him from growing as his friends did. Miguel remained small for as long as he lived. As an adult, he stood just five feet two inches tall.

But there was also much joy in Miguel's young life. There was the love of his parents and his sister Juana. There was the good feeling of helping his father in the fields. And the fun of tending the family's sheep and goats.

His body was frail, yes. But there was nothing frail about Miguel's spirit. Early in life, he learned a great lesson. His mother, Margarita, taught him that he must never give in to his illnesses. He must pay no attention to them. He must get back to work and play as soon as possible. Margarita helped him build an inner toughness that would serve him well in the years to come.

And so, Miguel never stayed in bed for long. He made himself get up and go outside. With his friends, he climbed trees and poked his way into dark caves. He went down to the docks at Petra to watch the fishing boats come and go.

And there was nothing frail about the boy's mind. He proved to be a fine student when he began attending the village school. His teachers were priests. They belonged to a religious group known as the Franciscan order. It had been formed 500 years earlier in Italy by St. Francis of Assisi. Again and again, his teachers saw Miguel stand at the head of his class.

He was such a good student that he was able to go to the university when he was just fourteen years old. The school was located at Las Palmas, the island's largest city. Miguel quickly impressed everyone there with his excellent classwork.

TWO GREAT DREAMS

Though he studied hard, Miguel did not give all his time to his books. There were hours when he sat thinking of two great dreams that were taking shape within him.

The first came from his early schooling under the

Franciscans. They had spoken much of St. Francis and the wonderful work he had done with the poor. Miguel loved the gentle saint and now dreamed of becoming a Franciscan priest.

His second dream went back to the days when he would wander down to the docks at Petra. There, he had heard many a sailor speak of voyages across the Atlantic Ocean to the New World. He had heard them talk of Spain's great possession, Mexico, with its mountains and deserts. He had listened to their tales of the Indians who lived there in poverty. He wanted to go to Mexico and work among the Indians, just as St. Francis had worked among the poor so long ago.

Miguel's dreams started to come true in 1729, when he was sixteen. He joined the Franciscan order and began his studies for the priesthood. He was ordained a priest eight years later, in 1737. He was now twenty-four years old. But he was no longer Miguel José Serra. As a priest, he took a new name for himself. He chose the name in honor of the monk who had assisted St. Francis for many years— the hard-working Brother Juniper. Miguel was now Father Junipero Serra.

Retrato del Rev. Padre Fray Junípero Serra Apos
la Alta California, tomado del original que se conserva
Convento de la Santa Cruz de Querétaro.

A portrait depicting Father Junipero Serra as he appeared during his years in Mexico.

IN THE NEW WORLD

One of his dreams had come true. But what of the dream of Mexico? It did not come true for another twelve years. During that time, he was a teacher of religion at the University of Las Palmas. All the while, he dreamed of the New World.

Then, suddenly, his life changed. In 1749, the Franciscan order sent twenty-two new missionaries to Mexico. A delighted Father Serra was among their number when their ship sailed westward in August. Fighting heavy winds for much of the time, the vessel made its way to the far side of the Atlantic by late October. It entered the Caribbean Sea, pressed on, and came to the east coast of Mexico. Junipero Serra went ashore on January 1, 1750.

But his journey was not yet done. The final destination was Mexico City. Ahead lay an overland trek of 250 miles. Father Serra's companions mounted burros for the trip, but he shook his head when offered one of the animals. He remembered that St. Francis had never made an animal carry him. He would do just as St. Francis had done. He would walk—and would go on doing so wherever he went in the New World.

The journey to Mexico City first took the priests across barren deserts and through dense jungles. Then they climbed into the mountains where the great city stood. Along the way, Father Serra suffered a painful injury.

It happened while he was passing through a jungle. Suddenly, he felt a sting in his leg. He looked down to see that he had been bitten—perhaps by a mosquito, perhaps by a snake. He never learned. Father Serra knew only that the sting became badly infected and developed into a pus-filled sore. It made walking a torture. But he refused to ride a burro. He limped the final miles to Mexico City.

The sore never completely healed. It gave the little priest great pain at times for the rest of his life. Whenever it caused trouble, he gritted his teeth and got on with his work. His mother's lesson of old was never forgotten.

Father Serra began nineteen years of hard work when he reached Mexico City. Some of those years were spent as a teacher at the local university. Others were passed as a missionary to an Indian tribe in the nearby Sierra Gorda Mountains. Then, in 1769, he was given a new task. It took him north to the greatest adventure of his life.

THE CALIFORNIA ADVENTURE

In Father Serra's day, the land called California was divided into two areas—Baja California and Alta California. In Spanish, *baja* means "lower" while *alta* is the word for "upper." Baja California was—and still is—the long, narrow peninsula stretching down along the coast of Mexico. It is separated from the Mexican mainland by the Gulf of California. Directly above it lay Alta California. Here was a vast region of deserts, forested mountains, and beaches. It would one day belong to the United States and be the state of California.

The Spanish had first explored Alta California back in the 1500s. Since then, they had claimed it to be one of their New World lands. But they had done nothing to settle the place. Now, in 1769, they were worried about it. It was being visited by Russian fur traders. The Spanish feared that the Russians might take control of the entire area.

To keep this from happening, they planned to send two expeditions northward. One would go by land, and the other by sea. They would meet at San Diego, a natural harbor long known to the Spanish. Then they would travel another 400 miles north to a second known spot—Monterey Bay. In both places, they would build forts. With soldiers guarding the two places, Spain would discourage the Russians from settling in California.

The land party was to be headed by the nobleman, Gaspar de Portolá. He would lead a troop of soldiers from Baja California. With him would be sixteen Franciscans. They would found missions and bring Christianity to the California Indians. Their leader was to be Father Serra.

The Portolá group began its march northward in March, 1769. As always, Father Serra refused to ride a burro. Wearing sandals and his simple gray robe, he limped along on his swollen leg for the entire journey.

Portolá and his men reached San Diego in July, 1769. Here, the marchers were joined by the sea expedition. And here, Father Serra founded his first California mission—Mission San Diego de Alcalá. It began as nothing more than a little wooden hut. Later, with Indian help, he and his missionaries fashioned a mission of adobe bricks.

The little hut almost proved to be not only his first but also his last mission. The priest very nearly lost his life there a few weeks later.

Mission San Diego de Alcalá as it looks in our century. This was

the first mission founded in California by Father Serra.

ATTACK!

His narrow escape came after the two groups had built a fort at San Diego. They then headed north to Monterey Bay. Along with a few soldiers, Father Serra was left behind to work at his mission. He soon found that the local Indians wanted nothing to do with him. They were angry at having strangers in their land. Their anger burst its bonds early one morning. Armed with bows and arrows, they attacked the small fort.

Father Serra had just finished saying mass. All about him, the Spanish soldiers dashed for their muskets. Angry shouts and the sound of gunshots filled the air. Arrows flew into the tiny hut. They barely missed the priest.

The attack lasted just a few minutes. The Indians with their primitive weapons were no match for the Spanish muskets. They gathered up their wounded and fled.

The Spanish soldiers wanted to take revenge for the assault. But Father Serra said that the attackers must be forgiven. He let the Indians know that he would tend their wounds. Slowly, they began coming to the mission for treatment. The priest's gentle care marked the start of friendship between the Indians and the Spanish.

NEW MISSIONS

In Father Serra's day, about 150,000 Indians lived in California. They were divided into many tribes. The priest found them to be strong and intelligent. They were excellent hunters of game and seafood. Between 1770 and 1782, Father Serra traveled among these people and founded his missions. Sometimes his trips were made by sea. More often, he walked on his throbbing leg. Two or three Franciscan fathers usually went with him. As soon as he picked a spot for a mission and saw the work on it started, he would leave his companions in charge and move on.

In all, after completing his work at San Diego, the priest founded another eight missions. Still standing today, his nine missions are:

Mission:	Founded:	Location:
San Diego de Alcalá	July, 1769	In the present-day city of San Diego

Mission:	Founded:	Location:
San Carlos Borromeo (known now as Mission Carmel)	June, 1770	A few miles south of Monterey Bay, at the city of Carmel
San Antonio de Padua	July, 1771	About 100 miles southeast of Monterey Bay
San Gabriel Archangel	September, 1772	About 50 miles east of today's city of Los Angeles
San Luis Obispo	September, 1776	About 100 miles south of Monterey Bay
San Francisco de Assis (known now as Mission Dolores)	October, 1776	In the present-day city of San Francisco
San Juan Capistrano	November, 1776	About 50 miles south of Los Angeles
Santa Clara de Asis	January, 1777	About 60 miles south of San Francisco
San Buenaventura	March, 1782	In the present-day city of Ventura

Father Serra was sixty-eight years old when Mission San Buenaventura was founded. He had been in the New World for thirty-two years. The work of those years had weakened his always frail health. He was now very ill. His leg was in constant pain. There was a growth on his chest that made it hard for him to breathe. The little priest retired to the mission at Monterey. It had long served as his headquarters. From there, he kept track of the work being done at the missions.

A FINAL JOURNEY

In 1783, Father Serra realized that his life was drawing to a close. Wanting to see his missions once again before death came, he started on a 500-mile walk that took him to all nine. His fellow priests were sure that he would never live through the trip. He proved them completely wrong.

Though a humble man, he could not help but be proud of how well the missions were doing. Most had been founded with great difficulty because the Indians had been angry at having strangers in their midst. Mision San Luis Obispo had been attacked and set afire by flaming arrows. There had been a second assault on San Diego, this one launched by

1,000 attackers. But, everywhere, the Franciscan fathers had slowly won the Indians over. Each year had seen more and more Indians come to the missions. There, they learned about Christianity and were taught how to farm.

With their help, each mission had taken shape. In general, each was built in the form of a quadrangle. To one side of the quadrangle stood the stone and adobe mission church with its bell tower and great altar. The church contained paintings and statues from Mexico and Spain. Next to it stood the *convento*, the building in which the missionaries lived. The other sides of the quadrangle were taken up by workshops, storerooms, a hospital, and rooms for the Indians who lived at the mission.

The fields around each mission were busy places. When Father Serra had first arrived, the Indians had been fine hunters and fishermen. But they had often gone hungry because they did not know how to raise food. His priests taught them to farm and they now raised livestock and a wide variety of fruits and vegetables. Much of what they produced was shipped to Mexico and Spain. The shipments marked the start of a trade with the outside world that goes on to this day in California.

Each day at a mission began at dawn. Mass was said and hymns were sung. Breakfast followed, with *atole* (a porridge made of cornmeal) being served to the Indians. Then came the day's work in the fields and workshops. Wagons and plows were built in the workshops, along with the red adobe tiles needed to keep the mission roofs in repair. At noon, everyone sat down to a lunch of *pazole* (a thick soup of wheat, corn, and meat). The day closed at sunset with prayers. Evenings were given to religious instruction.

A weary but happy Father Serra completed his walk in early 1784. He returned to Monterey and worked on for a few months. But he grew weaker each day. At last, he could no longer abide by the lesson his mother had once taught him. He took to his bed. Death came on August 28, 1784. In three months, he would have been seventy-one years old.

A PLACE IN HISTORY

Father Serra's work did not end with his death. Between 1787 and 1823, his fellow Franciscans went on to build another twelve missions, giving California twenty-one missions in all. When Mexico freed itself from Spain in the 1820s, it took control of California. But it forgot about the missions and allowed them to fall into ruin. Later, after California had become a part of the United States, they were restored. They are today among the state's most treasured landmarks.

And Father Serra is today one of the state's most important historical figures. He helped to bring western civilization to the region. In doing so, he paved the way for the future settlement of California. The work done in the mission fields started California on the road to becoming one of the richest farming areas on the North American continent.

Finally, when people from all over the world began to settle in California in the 1800s, many made their way to the mission sites. They wanted to enjoy the company of the people already there. It was around the missions that some of California's greatest cities first took shape—among them, San Diego, Los Angeles, Ventura, Santa Barbara, Monterey, and San Francisco.

The little priest whose father thought he would die just minutes after being born had not only lived a long life but won a lasting place in history.

CHAPTER TWO

John Charles Frémont

AS a youth, he did not look like someone who would spend much of his life in the wilds. He did not have the rugged features of the outdoorsman. Rather, he was a handsome boy with soft brown eyes and dark curly hair. His speech was quiet.

But his lean and muscular body was meant for the wilds. So was his courage. And so was his love of the outdoors. Together, they made him one of the most important explorers in American history. His name was John Charles Frémont.

A SOUTHERN BOYHOOD

Frémont was born at Savannah, Georgia, on January 21, 1813. His father was an artist who had come to the United States from France as a young man. The child's mother, Anne, was a member of a wealthy Virginia family.

The boy's earliest years were spent in various southern cities—wherever his father could find work. The traveling ended in 1818 when his father died just a few weeks after Frémont's sixth birthday. Anne and her son then settled in the city of Charleston, South Carolina.

Frémont always remembered the South Carolina years as happy ones. He enjoyed school and did so well that he was able to enter the College of Charleston at age sixteen. But even more enjoyable were the days he shared with the two sons and daughter of a neighbor family. The future explorer constantly stole away with them to roam the countryside.

All this fun, however, got Frémont into trouble while he was attending the College of Charleston. He had enrolled in 1828 to study civil engineering. But, one year, he stayed away from class too often to go adventuring with his three friends. His grades plunged. He was expelled from school.

For a time, Frémont did not know what to do with himself. Then, in 1833, he got a job aboard the U.S. warship *Natchez*. He had always been good at mathematics while at school. Now he was to coach the ship's crew in the subject during a cruise to South America. Frémont was twenty years old at the time.

OFFICER AND EXPLORER

The cruise lasted for three years. It was followed by another adventure when Frémont returned home in 1836. A railroad was being planned to run from Charleston to Cincinnati, Ohio. The young man spent several months in the wilderness with the army engineers who were surveying the planned route.

Frémont's work on the survey so impressed his superiors that they made him a second lieutenant in the army. Then they told him that he was going on an expedition with the famous French explorer, Joseph Nicholas Nicollet. The U.S. government was sending Nicollet to the wilds along the upper Mississippi River. Little was known about the region. Nicollet was to learn about the living conditions there. The information would be of help to a growing number of farmers who were interested in settling the area. Frémont was to be his assistant.

The expedition ventured far up the river and into

the present-day state of Minnesota. The new lieutenant drew maps of every spot he visited. He made friends with the Sioux Indians. He helped Nicollet study the plants, trees, and wildlife of the area. The journey lasted for two years. By the time it ended in 1839, Frémont was a seasoned explorer.

An adventure of a different kind now awaited the twenty-six-year-old traveler. He went to Washington, D.C., to help Nicollet write a report on their expedition. There, he met and fell in love with young Jessie Benton, the daughter of Senator Thomas Hart Benton of Missouri. They were married in 1841.

The marriage proved to be a happy one. Jessie gave her husband four children—two boys and two girls—and proved to be a great help to him in his work. Senator Benton also helped Frémont. It was with the Senator's aid that the explorer received his next assignments—the most important of his life. They took him all the way to the Pacific coast and gave him a lasting place in the history of California.

TO THE SOUTH PASS

In the early 1840s, pioneering families were beginning to head westward from the Mississippi.

Their destination was the Pacific coast. They planned to establish farms in the lush Oregon country north of California. Senator Benton and a number of other men in the U.S. Congress happily watched the movement. They wanted to see the Far West settled by Americans so that it could one day be made a part of the nation.

But they were also worried. The settlers were using maps that had been made by "mountain men"—the hunters and trappers who had lived in the western wilds for years. Though the mountain men knew the land well, they were not good mapmakers. Their maps were crude and often far from accurate. The settlers had to have accurate maps for a safe journey.

And so the Congress decided to send an expedition west. It would map the route taken by the settlers from the Mississippi to a point in the Rocky Mountains called the South Pass. The Pass was an opening that enabled travelers to move through the Rockies without struggling over towering peaks.

With Senator Benton's help, Frémont was named to head the expedition. The explorer quickly hired the hunters, mapmakers, and general helpers who would accompany him. Then, kissing Jessie fare-

Jessie Benton Frémont at her home in northern California. She assisted her husband in many ways throughout their marriage.

well, he headed for the Mississippi. On his arrival, he came upon a young man with ice-blue eyes. The man said that he knew the country ahead well. He wanted to serve as the expedition's guide. Frémont wasted no time in employing him when the stranger mentioned his name. He was Christopher "Kit" Carson, one of the most famous of all frontiersmen.

With Frémont and Carson riding at its head, the expedition left the Mississippi in early 1842. The party moved slowly westward, drawing maps and studying the nature of the land all along the way. Bands of Sioux Indians were sighted from time to time. The explorers had heard that the Sioux were hostile toward the whites invading their territory. They were constantly ready for an attack. It never came.

Frémont reached the South Pass in August. He found it to be a wide, gently rising break in the mountains. All around him were rugged peaks. Dead ahead lay a series of peaks known as the Wind Mountains. He picked the most towering of their number and climbed to its crest with several men. He was sure that he had bested the highest of the Wind Mountains. Today, we know it to be the second highest in the Wind range. It bears the explorer's name—Frémont Peak.

With his work done, Frémont headed home. But he was on the trail again the following year, in 1843. This time, he was to map the rest of the westward route—right to the Oregon settlements.

CLEAR ACROSS THE CONTINENT

As usual, Frémont and his men set out from the Mississippi River in the spring. With Kit Carson at his side, he made his way through the Rockies and came down into Oregon country. The journey ended near Fort Vancouver on the Pacific coast.

Frémont now said there was more work to do. He led his men south toward California. They hiked into the towering Sierra Nevada Mountains that stretch down the border of Nevada and California. Here, they lived through a terrible adventure.

Winter and its snow caught the party high in the mountains. Frémont knew that the men would die if they made camp and tried to sit out the freezing months. And so he aimed them toward the warm Sacramento valley in northern California. For weeks, they gasped in the thin air that cut into their lungs like an ice-coated knife. They plunged through blizzards that froze their faces, hands, and feet. Their supplies ran low.

But, at long last, they came out of the Sierras and into the snow-free Sacramento valley. They made camp there for the rest of the winter. Then, in the spring of 1844, they headed eastward. Frémont was back home late in the year.

With Jessie's help, Frémont immediately wrote a book about his western adventures. When published, the book sold thousands of copies. Many were purchased by people eager to settle in the West. Frémont had been well known because of his ealier explorations. The book now made him one of the most famous men of the day. He was known everywhere as "The Pathfinder."

WAR CLOUDS AND A NEW JOURNEY

Frémont was sent back to California soon after completing his book. He carried secret government orders. They had to do with the fact that Mexico and the United States were getting ready to go to war over the vast area of Texas.

Texas had a long and interesting history. It had first belonged to Spain. Then, when the people of Mexico broke free of their Spanish rulers in the 1820s, it became a Mexican province. In the 1830s, the white settlers in Texas rebelled against the Mexican government. Their uprising was a success. They declared Texas to be independent in 1836. They wanted it to be made a part of the United States.

Finally, in 1845, Congress passed a resolution that added Texas to the United States. The new state stretched all the way to the Rio Grande River. This angered Mexico. Mexico accused the U.S. of taking more land than the Texas settlers had won in their uprising. It was land that still belonged to Mexico.

Mexico also felt that the American leaders wanted to grab its other two provinces on the North American continent—New Mexico and California—so that the United States would extend from coast to coast. The tensions between the two neighbors had grown so great that a war was at hand.

Frémont and sixty-two men rode west in late 1845. His orders were to fight should the war break out. On reaching northern California, he was met by General José Castro of the Mexican army. Castro suspected that the explorer had come to cause trouble and ordered him to leave the territory. At first, Frémont refused. Then he saw that his force was far outnumbered by Castro's troops. It would do the United States no good to have all his men killed. He withdrew and headed for Oregon.

TWO RIDDLES

At this point, two puzzling events took place. First, as the explorer was moving into Oregon, a horseman galloped into camp one night. He handed Frémont a message from Washington, D.C. To this day, no one knows what that message said. Did it tell Frémont that the Mexican War was finally about to erupt? Or did it have anything at all to do with the war? No one can say. Only one thing is known. As soon as Frémont read the message, he turned his men south again.

Second, the Bear Flag Revolt took place soon after he arrived back in California. In May, 1846, the white settlers who lived just north of San Francisco rose against the Mexican general, Mariano Vallejo. They attacked Vallejo's headquarters at the small town of Sonoma, put his troops to flight, and took him prisoner. Then they pulled down the Mexican flag and raised one of their own in its place. It was a white flag with a brown bear and two gold stars enblazoned on it. The settlers proclaimed the area all around to be a new nation—the California republic. They planned to ask Washington to make their nation a part of the United States.

What is so puzzling about all this? It is that Frémont's men took no part in the revolt, even though they were camped near Sonoma at the time. But many historians believe that the presence of the armed band encouraged the settlers to rebel. Others believe that Frémont secretly urged the settlers to move against Vallejo. Perhaps the message had ordered him to do so. But, like the message itself, Frémont's part in the Bear Flag Revolt has always been a mystery.

WAR

There is no mystery, however, about what happened next. The Mexican War broke out in 1846. (Actually, it started just before the Bear Flag Revolt, but the news did not reach California until later.) There was fighting in Texas. Washington, D.C., was laying plans to invade Mexico. A flotilla of American warships sailed up to the California coast. In command was Commodore Robert F. Stockton.

Stockton called Frémont to his headquarters, gave him the rank of major, and placed him in command of a battalion of American volunteers known as "The Californians." Because of the Bear Flag Revolt and other rebellious actions, northern California was pretty much under American control. Only the southern area remained firmly in Mexican hands. Its chief military post was located at the small town of Los Angeles and was under the command of General Castro, the man who had ordered Frémont to leave the territory. Stockton told Frémont that the two of them were going to attack Castro.

On August 17, 1847, Frémont entered dusty little Los Angeles ahead of Stockton's force. Marching with his men was a brass band. Not a Mexican shot was fired at their approach. Nor was there an enemy shot when the invaders raised the American flag above the town square. The reason: Castro and his troops had fled to the nearby mountains.

It was, however, a short-lived victory. Castro attacked the next month and drove the Americans out. Frémont was back in northern California at the time. He was unable to return in time to help retake the town. That job was done by General Stephen B. Kearney, who had brought a force in from New Mexico.

TENSE MOMENTS

The Mexican War ended in 1848, with Texas, New Mexico, and California in U.S. hands. By then, Frémont had reached a tense moment in his life.

On coming to California, *both* Commodore Stockton and General Kearney carried orders to conquer the territory and form an American government there. The two began to argue over who was actually in command of the region. Frémont angered Kearney by siding with the Commodore. The General's anger turned to fury when Frémont refused to obey any of his orders.

It was a fury that cost Frémont dearly. Kearney won the dispute and Stockton departed. The general immediately charged the explorer with mutiny and disobedience. Frémont was sent to Washington to face a military trial—a court-martial.

The court-martial found Frémont guilty and ordered him to leave the army. President James K. Polk, however. cancelled the punishment because of the explorer's services to the nation. But Frémont was too angry to remain in the army. He resigned. He was a lieutenant colonel at the time.

THE YEARS GOOD AND BAD

His resignation marked the end of Frémont's great days as an explorer. In 1848 and again in 1853, he

John C. Frémont in uniform during the Civil War. By this time, he had completed the most important works of his life.

headed expeditions to the West. One ended in tragedy when winter caught him in the Rockies and took the lives of eleven of his men. The other expedition tried to find a railroad route south of the Rockies to the Pacific coast—and failed.

But this is not to say that the years were without their successes. Frémont purchased a large tract of land in Mariposa, a region in the Sierras above the San Joaquin valley. He and Jessie went to live there with their children. During the California gold rush, the yellow metal was found on their property and the Frémonts became a wealthy family. Then, when California became a state in 1850, the explorer served a term as one of its Senators to the U.S. Congress. He returned to the army during the Civil War and was given the rank of general. Finally, in 1864, he ran for the presidency against Abraham Lincoln. He withdrew from the race before the election.

The years following the Civil War were not good ones for Frémont. Because of some unwise business dealings, he lost the family fortune and the home at Mariposa. Though he served as governor of the Territory of Arizona from 1878 to 1883, his fame was gradually forgotten. He and Jessie lived quietly in Los Angeles and then in New York City. At times, they were so hard-pressed for money that she supported Frémont by writing newspaper articles.

Frémont's health declined in his last years. Frail and bent, the man who had been called "The Pathfinder" died on July 13, 1890, at age seventy-seven. Jessie lived until 1902.

The people of the late 1800s may have forgotten Frémont. But, today, he is remembered throughout the West. His expeditions did much to open the Far West to settlement. And his part in the Mexican War helped to set California on the road to becoming an American state.

CHAPTER THREE

John A. Sutter

THERE was a cold rain that January day in 1848. But it did not dampen John A. Sutter's spirits. He was in a fine mood as he sat in his office and thought about the past nine years. He had worked wonders since coming here to northern California's Sacramento valley.

For one, he had obtained more than 48,000 acres of land. For another, he had built a fine trading post on that land. The post bore his name. It was called Sutter's Fort.

The post was always busy because it stood on the main route that American settlers took to northern California. Its stores sold them food, tools, and clothing as they passed by. Its workshops repaired their wagons. Further, some 13,000 cattle grazed on the surrounding acres. Other acres were planted with wheat and vegetables. Still others were covered with forests that gave Sutter a fine supply of timber.

He smiled. His lands and fort were making him what he had always longed to be—an important businessman. Then he shook his head. No, he told himself, he was not just a businessman. He had become something far greater. His lands were his realm. He was a *king*.

Sutter did not know it, but this day was to be a terrible one. At that moment, one of his workers was riding hard to the fort from the nearby Sierra foothills. The man was bringing news that would mark the end of all that Sutter had worked for in his life.

A LITTLE KNOWN BACKGROUND

Little is known about the early part of Sutter's life. Only a few things can be said for certain. The future "king" was born on February 15, 1803, at the town of Kandern in southwest Germany. His was a family of Swiss papermakers whose last name was spelled Suter. The newcomer was christened

Johann August. A few months later, his parents moved to Basel, Switzerland.

Sutter always said that he went to a good school at Basel and then attended a military academy. He also said that he had been an officer in the Swiss army. But his stories of his early life are not to be trusted. It has been found that the academy never existed and that he was never a soldier. The fact is, he was always saying things to make himself seem important.

There were times, for example, when he passed himself off as a former officer in the Prince of Prussia's army. And, as a young man, he changed his name to John Sutter and stretched his middle name from August to the grander-sounding Augustus.

Then what was the truth of the man's early life? It was that he worked as a clerk in various stores after completing his schooling. He was employed in a grocery store at the time he married Annette Dujeld in 1826. They opened a shop that sold various kinds of cloth. The shop failed and had to be closed in 1831.

The loss of the shop was very embarrassing to the man who always wanted people to think him successful and important. So was the fact that he was left deep in debt. Worst of all, he and Annette began fighting over their lack of money.

Sutter found that he could not bear all his problems. And so, without warning, he left his wife and three children. At age thirty-one, he fled to the United States.

ESCAPE WEST

Sutter arrived in New York City in July, 1834. For the next five years, he traveled far. First, he went to New Mexico for a stay. Next, he ventured northwest to Oregon country. Then he sailed to the Hawaiian Islands.

In all these places, Sutter worked as a trader. He called himself "Captain Sutter." Many people believed his fairy tales of adventure as an army officer. One such person was King Kamehameha of Hawaii. The king offered Sutter a post in the Hawaiian army. The make-believe soldier wisely refused the job.

The Islands were Sutter's last stop before coming to California. In 1839, he took a ship from Honolulu to the tiny village of Yerba Buena, which would one day be the city of San Francisco. He then purchased several small boats, sailed them across San Francisco Bay, and entered the Sacramento River. He was headed for the Sacramento valley.

Sutter had dreamed of the valley ever since his days in Oregon country. He had heard trappers and hunters speak of it in glowing terms. It was wide-open country, they said. Only Indians lived there. Its soil was rich. It boasted countless wild animals. Further, in growing numbers, American families were coming west to settle in California. They were crossing the valley on the way to their final destinations.

Sutter became sure of two things. Any man who planted the valley could become a rich farmer. And any man who built a trading post for the passing families could make a fortune as a merchant. He was determined to be both men.

More than a dozen white and Mexican men went on the river journey with Sutter. They were adventurers whom he had hired in San Francisco. There were also ten Kanaka Indians. They had come with Sutter from Hawaii. With the Kanakas at the oars, the boats glided along the Sacramento River.

John A. Sutter as he looked during the last years of his life.

Everyone watched the shore for signs of trouble. The local Indians were said to be hostile to strangers. But not an Indian was sighted—that is, not until the boats reached a point near where the city of Sacramento stands today.

It was then that some 200 Indians appeared at the river's edge. Waving spears and clubs, they yelled angrily at the strangers. Fear broke out in the boats. Sutter's men demanded that he turn and row to safety. Sutter shook his head. He had made friends with many Indians on his trip to Oregon and felt he could do the same here. He ordered the boats to land.

Though he had never been a soldier, Sutter knew how to act like one. He put his pistols aside as a sign of peace. Then he went ashore and walked proudly to the Indians. He spoke to them in Spanish. He hoped that some had lived at the California missions and understood the language. Relief poured through him when two braves stepped forward. They replied in Spanish. Calmly, Sutter explained that he had come to live among their people as a friend. The anger went out of the dark faces. Sutter was allowed to go on his way. The Indians promised to work for him when he built his trading post.

NEW HELVETIA

The journey ended a few miles later. Sutter called a halt alongside a plain that stretched away in gentle rolls to the Sierra foothills some thirty miles in the distance. He christened the surrounding land New Helvetia in honor of his home country. (*Helvetia* means Switzerland). Then he set about building his post.

It started as a cluster of tents. Soon, he replaced them with wooden huts. Next, crops were planted. Then Sutter opened his stores for the passing settlers. In the beginning, he saw just a few dozen families a year. But he knew the number would grow as more and more Americans came to the Far West.

California was still in Mexican hands at this time. While the post was taking shape, Sutter made several trips to the city of Monterey. The territorial governor, Juan Bautista Alvarado, had his headquarters there. The newcomer found Alvarado happy to have him in the territory. The governor felt that Sutter was helping Mexico by bringing civilization to one of California's untamed areas. A close friendship grew up between the two. Sutter became a citizen of Mexico, and Alvarado helped him obtain a land grant from the Mexican government.

Given to the trader was the land stretching away in all directions from his post—a total of 48,818 acres. Sutter was also made the representative of the Mexican government in the valley. He could hardly believe his good luck. He had received two wonderful gifts—a government position and a farming kingdom all his own. The year was 1841. Sutter had been in California just two years. At age thirty-eight, he had finally become the important man he had always wanted to be.

Sutter hurried back to New Helvetia. He planted new crops and began to increase his herds. As a representative of Mexico, he turned his post into a fort that would protect the interests of his new country in the valley. Sutter called the place "The Fort of New Helvetia." In time, it became known simply as "Sutter's Fort." And, because it stood on the main route that the American settlers took to northern California, it soon became the most famous trading post in America.

The fort struck everyone who saw it as a magnificent sight. At its center was a large two-story adobe building. Within were various offices and

Sutter's living quarters. A courtyard, 300 feet long by 160 feet wide, stretched away to all sides of the building. The courtyard was surrounded by walls made of adobe and timber. They were eighteen feet high and three feet thick. Inside these walls were workshops, storerooms, living quarters for Sutter's army of workers, and stores where visiting settlers could purchase food and supplies. There were also workshops outside the fort. In time, Sutter's workers were operating a slaughterhouse, tannery, blanket factory, carpenter shop, and blacksmith shop.

The man who had never been a soldier ran his post in firm military fashion. He chose the best of the valley Indians and turned them into well-trained soldiers. They and all his workers were awakened each dawn with a bugle call. While the workers labored in the shops and fields, the Indian troopers drilled and stood guard at the heavily timbered main gate.

A CHANGE OF SIDES

No sooner was the fort built than the Mexican authorities began to worry about Sutter. They knew that war with the United States was approaching

Sutter's Fort today. It stands within a residential district in Sacramento, capital of California. Restored by the state, it is open to

over Mexico's territories on the North American continent, among them California. Though Sutter had become a Mexican citizen, they wondered if he would remain loyal when the fighting broke out. They feared he would change sides and support the United States.

the public and features displays of tools, vehicles, furnishings, and clothing used in Sutter's day.

Their fears proved to be correct. Sutter recognized the great strength of the United States. Also, most of his business came from the U.S. settlers. He wanted to keep their friendship. He sided with the Americans and let them use the fort during the war. The fort was never the scene of fighting.

The Mexican War lasted from 1846 to 1848. It ended in an American victory. Even before then, however, California was safely in U.S. hands. This brought more settlers in from the East than ever before. Sutter had once seen just a few dozen families in a year's time. Now up to 200 were beginning to stop by the fort each year. They purchased his goods and paid for the services given by his workshops. There was a growing demand for his cattle, timber, and farm crops in the towns taking shape throughout California. Though always faced with many bills for salaries and supplies, Sutter was becoming a very wealthy king indeed.

Then came that day of thin, icy rain.

THE SECRET VISIT

It was January 28, 1848. One of Sutter's workers—James Marshall—rode down from the nearby Sierra foothills. Rain poured from Marshall's buckskins as he strode into his employer's office. In a hoarse whisper, he demanded that they talk in a place where they could not be overheard.

Puzzled, Sutter led the way to a small room away from his busy offices. Two weeks back, he had sent

Marshall to the foothills. The man was to help build a sawmill. Trees were being felled in the area and the mill was needed to cut them into boards for shipment to the fort. Now he watched Marshall move to a table and bring out a leather pouch. Marshall tore the pouch open. Flecks and tiny lumps of yellow metal fell out. Sutter's eyes widened. The little things looked like gold.

As Sutter bent over the metal, Marshall told his story. A few days ago, he had noticed some glittering flecks in the water pouring into the mill's sluice box. He had then found several lumps of the shiny stuff in the waterway leading to the box. Certain that he had found a rich vein of gold, he had hurried to his employer. He had kept his news secret so that Sutter's workers would not run off and go looking for quick riches for themselves.

Sutter did not know if the metal was actually gold. It could have been pyrite, the worthless yellow mineral that was called "fool's gold." There was only one way to find out. He tested the metal for proper weight and softness. Then he coated it with nitric acid. The metal did not change color.

Sutter's eyes were now wide with excitement. This was indeed gold. A high quality gold. He was going to be the wealthiest king ever—if only the find could remain a secret.

GOLD AND DISASTER

But the secret could not be kept. Word leaked out of a rich discovery in the Sierras. It made its way to the East Coast and then to the rest of the world—and triggered one of the greatest gold rushes in history.

Instantly, thousands of men from every walk of life—from doctors and lawyers to farmers and store clerks—headed for California. Traveling by wagon train and ship, they swarmed in from everywhere—from the American East and Midwest and from Europe, South America, Australia, and China. Those who came by ship landed at the village of Yerba Buena, which had now been given the name San Francisco in honor of the mission that Father Junipero Serra had built there. In early 1848, the town had boasted just 250 inhabitants. By mid-1849, more than 40,000 gold seekers had come pouring in. Thousands more were still on their way. San Francisco had become a crowded city of wooden hotels, saloons, restaurants, gambling halls, and shops crammed with everything needed for mining.

From San Francisco, the newcomers headed into the gold fields that were now spreading for miles through the Sierras. Thousands hiked across Sutter's "kingdom." A great number halted to dig up his earth and pan his streams. Sutter tried to stop them. He shouted that the land and its hidden treasures were his. But his words did no good. There were simply too many intruders for him to handle.

Then, when many failed to find the wealth they sought, they settled on his land to start farms. Worse, his workers left him and went gold hunting. Left behind to tend his fields and the fort were just a few loyal Indians. Soon his crops dwindled, helped along by a flood that swept across his acres in 1849. His shops began to close as the town of Sacramento took shape nearby. It was soon crowded with stores that provided people with all the goods that once only he had sold.

A dazed Sutter watched his kingdom come crashing down. Within two years after that rainy January day in 1848, the kingdom lay in ruins. Sutter was a poor man again—as poor as he had been when his shop in Switzerland had gone out of business so long ago. He had reigned as a monarch for little more than a decade. He left his fort and went to live at a farm he had built some years earlier in the foothills. Later he lived in the East. Left behind were empty and dusty shops and storerooms. Around them, the once-grand walls began to crumble.

THE TRAGIC FIGURE

John A. Sutter ranks as one of California's most tragic figures. Starting as a poor man, he rose to great heights, only to be cast down again. He remained a poor man from the day he left the fort to the end of his life.

Time and again after California became a state in 1850, he tried to win back some of his wealth. He did so by asking the U.S. Congress to pay him for his lost land and for the help his fort had given to so many settlers. Congress refused his requests, saying that he had received his acres from a foreign power. Thus, he had no claim against the U.S. government. In 1880, Sutter went to Washington, D.C., to make yet another appeal. He died there on June

17 before receiving an answer. He was seventy-seven years old.

Tragic though his end may have been, Sutter remains one of the most important figures in California history. First, he tamed a wilderness valley that became a major farming area. Second, he built a trading post that was considered the greatest of its day as it welcomed and assisted hundreds of passing settlers. Finally, the discovery of gold on his land caused the first truly great rush of people to California. The rush has continued to the present day and has made California the most heavily populated state in the nation.

CHAPTER FOUR

Henry Wells and. . . William G. Fargo

THERE is an odd fact about two of the most important men in California history. Neither ever lived in the state. Yet they gave California a giant company of stagecoaches, freight wagons, banking offices, and mail deliveries. The two men were Henry Wells and William G. Fargo, the founders of Wells Fargo & Company.

HENRY WELLS

Born December 12, 1805, Henry Wells was raised at Thetford, a small Vermont town. As a young man, he moved to New York State and went to work for Harnden's Express. In keeping with the word *express*—which means "rapid conveyance"—the company was in the business of making deliveries as swiftly as possible. It delivered all kinds of things, from letters and packages to merchandise and money.

Harnden's was just one of many such companies. They were all a great help to businesses and families in the time before today's systems of rapid communication and transportation came into being.

The slender Wells began as one of Harnden's deliverymen. He proved so good at his job that he was promoted to positions of greater responsibility. He also proved to be an ambitious man who wanted to be in business for himself. And so, in 1842, he formed his own express company with two friends. Close on its heels came a second firm, which he called Wells & Company. A third firm took shape in 1850—the American Express Company, today a giant operation doing business throughout the world.

By now, Wells was forty-five years old and a wealthy man. And, by now, he and William G. Fargo had been close friends for eight years.

WILLIAM G. FARGO

William George Fargo was thirteen years younger than Wells. The date of his birth was May 20, 1818. His birthplace was the city of Albany, New York.

After working as a railroad conductor, he took a job as an express company deliveryman. He went to work for Wells in 1842 when Wells formed his first company.

Fargo was a fine employee. His deliveries were very swift because he was an excellent horseman. He became such a valued worker that Wells made him a partner when Wells & Company was formed. Fargo became a high-ranking executive with American Express when that company took shape.

By 1852, the two friends were important businessmen in the East. They began to look to the West. Because of the gold rush that had started in 1848, northern California had become one of the busiest regions in the nation. Its many mining towns were all in need of food and supplies. They were being served by a number of express companies, some large and some small. But the region was so busy that the two men were certain it could use another. They decided that they must establish a company in the new state. On May 18, 1852, Wells Fargo & Company was established.

THE CALIFORNIA VISIT

The company's main office was located in New

York City. There, Wells and Fargo laid plans for their new venture.

First, they decided that the company would build offices in the many mining towns now dotting the Sierra Mountains. Then it would purchase gold from the miners, ship it down to San Francisco, and send it to New York. The company would make a profit by buying the gold for slightly less than it was worth in the East and then selling it or using it to make investments when it reached New York. Next, the company would provide a stagecoach service for travelers going to and from the gold fields. Finally, it would ship all types of needed goods from the East to San Francisco.

Two of the firm's top employees traveled to San Francisco in the spring of 1852. There, they opened the first Wells Fargo office in California. Henry Wells followed them a few weeks later. He wanted to visit the Sierra mining towns so that he could learn first-hand the problems that working among them might bring. His trek into the mountains netted him a number of fine ideas for the company. One of the first had to do with mail from home for the miners.

Wells learned that nearly all of the miners had come west alone, leaving their families safe at home. Their hope had been to "strike it rich" fast and

Henry Wells

William G. Fargo

return to give their loved ones a better life. Now they yearned for news of family and friends. But mail delivery was a problem because the miners were constantly on the move. They were always moving to new diggings when the earth failed to reveal its hidden wealth. They were often impossible for the U.S. Postal Service to find.

Wells decided that his company would take on an extra job. It would start a mail service. The service would carry letters for a slightly higher fee than the Postal Service charged. He was sure no one would mind the fee because of a plan that had come to mind. It was a plan to make the miners easy to find and thus insure that their mail reached them.

The plan called for a miner to leave his name at the local Wells Fargo office whenever he came into a new town. The name would be placed on a card that would be sent to the San Francisco office. Then, when mail arrived in San Francisco, the employees there would look up the miner's latest card and forward the letter to its proper destination. The system worked beautifully. It was used by countless families everywhere.

Wells soon reached another decision. He knew that the offices in the mining towns would need rugged safes to hold the gold dust purchased by the company. There was no other way to protect the gold before it was shipped off to the East. Now he decided that the offices would have to be more than buildings with safes in them. They would have to be actual banks.

He knew that not all miners wanted to sell their gold to the company. Some planned to take all or a portion of their dust home for everyone to see. Until then, they needed a place where it could be safely stored. Wells said that each company office would hold the gold dust for them, just as banks held money for their customers. The company would charge a small monthly fee for this service.

The system worked this way: A miner could store his dust in any Wells Fargo office. In return, he was given a slip of paper with the exact amount of the deposit written on it. He could then hand the slip in at any Wells Fargo office at any time and receive a like amount in gold. The company promised that it would be completely responsible for the deposit. If the gold were misplaced or stolen, Wells Fargo would make good the loss. The system proved so popular that the company was soon providing all types of banking services.

Stolen gold! Those two words haunted Wells throughout his trip and brought him to yet another decision. The company planned to have its offices place its gold in boxes that would be shipped down to San Francisco aboard stagecoaches and wagons. For much of the time, the shipments would be moving along wilderness trails. Those trails would make fine places for robberies.

Wells had good reason to fear robberies. The gold rush had attracted all types of men from over the world—from the very finest to the very worst. Among the latter were cutthroats, burglars, shady gamblers, and bandits. They had already robbed and cheated miners everywhere. The rich gold shipments were bound to be their next prey.

Wells set down two rules concerning the robberies that were sure to come. First, since much of the gold was to be shipped aboard stagecoaches, he issued orders to his drivers. If they were held up by bandits while carrying passengers, they were not to put up a fight. They were to hand over their "treasure boxes" without a word. This would protect the passengers. The passengers must always know that they were safe when traveling with Wells Fargo.

Second, no matter how small the amount taken, the company was to spare no expense in tracking down the robbers. By letting highwaymen know that they would pay dearly for their crimes, Wells hoped to discourage at least some robbery attempts.

Throughout its history, Wells Fargo never strayed from these rules. They made the company one of the most trusted firms of the day.

A Wells Fargo stagecoach, one of the most famous and familiar sights in California during the late 1800s.

THE GROWING COMPANY

When Wells returned to New York, his ideas were put into practice. The company quickly took shape. Wells Fargo offices were built in all the Sierra mining towns. In the smaller towns, the offices were one-room wooden affairs. Each had a safe. The larger towns had large buildings of brick and stone. The large offices boasted giant vaults with steel doors weighing more than a ton.

The job of starting the company was an awesome one. In itself, the building of all the offices was big enough. But added to it was the task of getting all the needed equipment into place. Stagecoaches and safes were shipped in from the East. So were the giant vault doors used in the larger offices. Horses for the stagecoaches and mules for freight wagons were rounded up from throughout the West.

On top of everything else, hundreds of employees had to be hired—from stage drivers and office workers to blacksmiths for shoeing the stagecoach teams and repairing the coaches.

But all this work paid fine dividends. Within a few years, Wells Fargo had extended its operations to all of California and then to areas beyond the state. Leaving its competitors behind, it became the leading express company not only in California but in the entire American West. It had more than 1,300 offices and the largest fleet of stagecoaches in the country. Yearly, it carried thousands of passengers, shipped tons of freight, and provided banking services for an army of customers.

STORIES AND MORE STORIES

As it grew, Wells Fargo wrote one of the most fascinating chapters in California history. It was a chapter filled with exciting stories. There were tales about the company's stage drivers. All of them were daredevils who went dashing along the roughest trails and through any sort of weather.

Among the best yarns was one told about driver Charles Watson. One day, his stage was robbed by several masked men. When the highwaymen rode off, Charles drove to the next town where he stopped at a hotel to let his frightened passengers rest. A little while later, two men entered and asked for a room for the night. They were dressed as miners, but Charley's eyes widened when he heard them speak. He recognized those voices. He had heard them coming from behind masks back on the trail. The driver quietly left and hunted up the local sheriff. The two men were soon under arrest.

There were also tales about the many items shipped by Wells Fargo. The company seemed willing to carry goods of any type. At one end of the scale, there were such delicacies as fresh oysters. At the other end was the giant steam engine that was hauled from Baltimore to Sacramento in 1861. Much freight was devoted to California's growing farm industry. Wells Fargo wagons hauled tons of wheat, vegetables, fruits, and meats to all parts of the state and to eastern markets. Also shipped were all types of industrial construction materials.

One industrial shipment ended in tragedy for the San Francisco office. In the mid-1850s, a crate arrived containing tin cans full of nitroglycerine, used in making dynamite. Because the substance was just recently invented, a worker had not yet learned how dangerous it was. He began to open the crate by pounding it with a hammer. There was an explosion that shook windows throughout San Francisco. The back wall of the office was blown away and six employees were killed.

For many, the very best of the Wells Fargo tales

concerned the bandits who harassed the company for years. For example, there were Richard Barter and Tom Bell. Though Barter had an evil-sounding nickname—Rattlesnake Dick—he was famous for his courtesy to passengers when relieving a stage of its treasure box. On the other hand, Bell headed a vicious gang that once shot a woman passenger during a holdup. The two bandits were tracked down by lawmen and killed.

The most famous of the highwaymen was the bandit nicknamed Black Bart. Tall and courteous, he was always well-dressed and kept his face covered with a flour sack that had two eye-holes cut in it. Bart plagued the company from 1875 to 1883. He robbed no fewer than twenty-eight coaches.

Bart's real name was Charles Boles. He had ventured west to find gold after serving as a Union soldier in the Civil War. When his search failed, he turned to crime. His nickname came from his habit of leaving notes at the scene of a robbery. The notes, often written in verse, were signed *Black Bart, the PO-8*. PO-8 meant "poet." Here is one of his best-known verses:

> Here I lay me down to sleep
> To wait the coming morrow,

Perhaps success, perhaps defeat
And everlasting sorrow.

Let come what will I'll try it on,
My condition can't be worse;
And if there's money in that box
'Tis munny in my purse.
                                    Black Bart, the PO-8

Unlike many of his fellow bandits, Bart worked alone. His method was to hide at the base of a hill and then, rifle in hand, step from the bushes and halt a stagecoach as it slowed for the coming climb. In a polite voice, he would order the driver to throw down the treasure box. On breaking it open with a small axe, he would take the gold and disappear back into the underbrush. Not once did he ever steal from the passengers.

Bart avoided capture for years because he was a fine outdoorsman. Carrying only his axe and a blanket roll, he moved swiftly and kept far ahead of his pursuers. His downfall came when a passenger fired a shot at him during a holdup and caused him to drop a handkerchief as he fled.

The handkerchief bore a laundry mark. Detectives in Wells Fargo's employ traced the mark to a San Francisco laundry and identified the owner of the handkerchief. When arrested, Bart turned out to be an elderly and respected citizen. He was sent to San Quentin prison for six years. Soon after completing his sentence, Bart disappeared, never to be seen again.

A CHANGING COMPANY

Though Wells Fargo did well until the early twentieth century, the company began to suffer during the late 1800s. Its passenger and freight business fell off when the first transcontinental railroad was completed in 1869 and linked the West and East with fast-moving trains. Then the company's mail business went down when the U.S. Postal Service began making faster deliveries and when the telegraph came into use. In the early 1900s, the company ended its stagecoach and mail services.

The early 1900s also saw Wells Fargo leave the banking business. The banking service was sold in 1905. The new owners kept the company name. Today, the Wells Fargo Bank is one of the largest banks in the West.

The original Wells Fargo company presently owns several firms. They perform a variety of business services. Three operate armored trucks that serve banks in the eastern United States. Another counts and wraps coins for banks in the New York City area.

FULL AND BUSY YEARS

Both Henry Wells and William G. Fargo were busy men throughout the final years of their lives. Both guided the work of their company by serving on its board of directors. Wells also served as president of his American Express Company from its formation in 1850 until his retirement in 1868. Fargo worked for American Express as an executive during those same years. He became the firm's president when Wells retired. Fargo continued as president until his death. He also served as mayor of Buffalo, New York, from 1862 to 1866.

While staying at Glasgow, Scotland, Wells died on December 10, 1878, just two days before his seventy-third birthday. Fargo followed him in death three years later. He died on August 3, 1881, at Buffalo. He was sixty-three years old.

Though they never lived in California, the two friends hold an honored place in its history. California was rapidly growing during the latter half of the nineteenth century. They did much to help that growth with their company and its various needed services.

In all, the two men did much more than assist the growth of the state. They hastened it.

CHAPTER FIVE

John Muir

HE was known as a mechanical wizard in the factory where he worked. But his wizardry did not save him from an accident one day. As he was repairing a circular saw, a steel file slipped from his hands. It flew into his right eye. The pain went over to his left eye. He was totally blind for several days.

The brief loss of his sight changed the young man's life. He was terrified because his greatest joy had been taken away. It was the joy of hiking through the woods to see the trees and plants. He made a decision. He would never be without that joy again. He would give up machinery. He would travel from now on and give his eyes to the study of nature wherever he went.

For all Americans who love the outdoors, his decision was a happy one. The young mechanic became one of the nation's leading naturalists and conservationists. His name was John Muir.

FROM SCOTLAND TO AMERICA

John Muir was born on April 21, 1838, at the town of Dunbar in eastern Scotland. His parents' names were Daniel and Ann. He was the third of their eight children. The boy had two brothers and five sisters.

John always remembered his mother as a gentle woman who enjoyed reading poetry. His memories of his father were of a loving but very strict parent. Daniel was quick to deliver a spanking whenever he caught his youngsters wasting their time or forgetting their chores.

Despite his father's strictness, John had a happy childhood. He early discovered his love of nature as he explored the fields around Dunbar. That love deepened when he began school and found some books containing stories and drawings of the vast wilderness areas in faraway America. They were areas blessed with thick forests and wonderful animals—bears, deer, buffalo, and soaring eagles. He wanted nothing more than to go there and see these marvels for himself.

It was a dream that suddenly came true in 1849, just before John's eleventh birthday. Daniel Muir ran a successful grain-and-food store. But he, too, wanted to move to the United States. He thought the new nation would offer his family a better life. One night, he rushed home with startling news. He had just sold his store. Everyone would soon be moving to—John could hardly believe his ears—America!

The move ended some months later near the small Wisconsin town of Portage. Here, the family built a house and began to farm the surrounding land. Here, John Muir happily roamed the outdoors and then, in his early teens, showed himself to be a mechanical wizard. Working late at night so that his farm chores would never go undone, he began to dream up and construct what the neighbors called "Muir's inventions."

"MUIR'S INVENTIONS"

There were many. John built thermometers, barometers, and tools to help with the farm work. But everyone agreed that his best things were his clocks. One was possibly the oddest and funniest alarm clock ever designed. It was attached to a device that jiggled the sleeper's bed at the hour for rising.

Just as strange was his "clock desk." Odd though it was, the desk served a very serious purpose. John could not go to school because he was needed at home to assist with the new farm's many chores. But, always hungry for knowledge, he was determined to have an education. He would be his own teacher. He built the desk to help him waste no time when he studied.

The desk stood nine feet tall. At its top was a wheel to which a mechanical arm was fastened. Several clocks caused the wheel to turn by means of a system of gears. Each time the wheel turned, the arm swept outward. It removed the top book from a stack of volumes on a shelf. Down it brought the book to a spot in front of John and then opened it to the page to be studied. He timed the clocks so that each book could be read for a certain number of minutes before being replaced by another. Whenever John sat down to his studies, he engaged in a race to keep up with the "clock desk."

The mechanical skills that made John's inventions possible served him well. They won him prizes at a Wisconsin State Fair. They impressed his teachers when, at last able to attend school, he entered the University of Wisconsin at age twenty-two. He remained at the university from 1860 to 1863. In the main, he studied botany and geology. Then, in 1866, his skills landed him a job in Indianapolis, Indiana. He went to work in a factory that manufactured the parts used in carriage wheels.

A year later, that steel file struck him in the eye and sent him off to a life of travel and nature study.

THE NEW LIFE BEGINS

The first trip of John Muir's new life was an ambitious one. On September 1, 1867, he left Indianapolis on a 1,000-mile walk to the Gulf of Mexico. Making notes and collecting plant specimens at every turn of the way, he explored the wild regions of Kentucky, North Carolina, Georgia, and Florida. Then, on arriving at the Gulf, he sailed to the island of Cuba for a brief stay.

Ambitious though the journey was, his next trip was even better. He booked passage to California in early 1868. The lanky twenty-nine-year-old traveler did not know it, but he was heading for the

JOHN MUIR · 89

state where he would spend the rest of his life and
win national fame.

The journey took Muir by sea to San Francisco.
No sooner did he arrive than he put the city behind
him. Eager to get back to the nature he loved, he
began hiking east through lands covered with wild
grass, forests, and flowers of every color. He stopped
once to earn some money tending sheep. Then came
the day when, some 150 miles from San Francisco,
he walked to the edge of a bluff in the Sierras. He
looked down and had his breath swept away.

Below him lay the deep Yosemite valley. He saw
streams running through meadowlands. There were
timber stands and small lakes and pools. There were
waterfalls. Surrounding all this beauty were granite
walls that rose straight up to heights of 3,000 to
4,000 feet. Beyond the valley stood the towering
Sierra peaks. Muir made his way down into the
valley. He thought it the most beautiful place he
had ever seen. He decided that he must make his
home here.

Muir remained for six years. For much of the
time, he lived in a cabin and earned money by
working for the owner of a hotel. The valley was
beginning to attract visitors from throughout Cal-

ifornia and was served by two hotels. He struck all
the visitors as an odd man—tall and rail thin, long
of stride, bearded, dressed always in coveralls, and
happy to be living by himself in his rough cabin.
They found him friendly and eager to talk about
nature. But they felt he always took greater pleasure
in rocks, trees, and plants than in people.

They had every reason to think as they did. On
his free days, Muir never failed to disappear. He
hurried into the wilds to explore every inch of the
valley and the Sierra mountains towering above it.
As a result of his wanderings, he developed a theory on how the valley had been formed eons ago.
It was a theory that was to win him his first taste
of fame.

MAN OF THE GLACIERS

At the time, geologists believed that the valley
had been formed by violent earthquakes. The quakes
had caused the ground to sink and create the valley
floor. And they had thrust giant rock formations
upward. The rocks had become the surrounding

A portrait of John Muir in the later years of his life.

granite walls. Muir agreed with these ideas. But he came to suspect that another force had also been at work.

His suspicions were aroused when he sighted gouges and deep scratches in the valley walls. Muir believed them to be scars left behind by vast sheets of moving ice and snow—glaciers. He found the very same markings in the nearby mountains. All this indicated one thing to him. Glaciers had come creeping down from the Sierras millions of years ago. Tearing away at the land, they had helped to form the valley.

He wrote several newspaper articles on his theory. But geologists scoffed at the whole idea. They said that there had never been glaciers in the Sierras. Not a one had ever been seen. Muir soon made them take back their words. On his trips into the mountains in the early 1870s, he found wide strips of torn ground that looked like the paths once taken by long-vanished glaciers. Then he began to stumble upon fields of ice that lay behind banks of dirt and stone. They looked exactly as if they were pushing the banks along toward the valley. In a two-year period, he discovered more than sixty such fields.

Muir was jubilant. He was sure that he had come upon the things that no one had ever before noticed in these mountains—glaciers. But he had to prove that they were actually glaciers and not merely snowbanks. He had to show that they *moved*. And so he planted five stakes on a white-sheeted mountainside east of the valley and left them there for six weeks. On his return, he found that they had all moved—for distances ranging from eleven to forty-seven inches. He was right! He had found a glacier! The other ice fields must also be glaciers. His theory had the proof it needed.

Hurrying to his desk, Muir wrote an article that made the geologists pay attention. His theory became very popular in the next years and was finally accepted as truth. With earthquakes and other natural forces, glaciers now share the responsibility for creating one of the world's most beautiful spots.

His theory won John Muir national fame and changed his life in two ways. First, he became a well-known writer because newspapers and magazines were always asking him for nature articles. Second, he moved back to the San Francisco Bay area to do his writing—and met Louie Wanda Strentzel. She was a dark-haired and quiet woman who was eight years his junior. Quiet though she was, Louie had a good business head and was very successful in running her family's fruit ranch near Martinez, a small town north of the city of Oakland. Muir fell in love with her.

FIGHTING FOR CONSERVATION

Muir courted Louie Wanda for several years before asking her to marry him. Their romance was constantly interrupted by his trips into the field. One summer, he hiked through the breathtaking redwood trees that stretch south for miles through the Sierras from a point below Yosemite valley. These giant trees, rising to heights of 300 feet, are now preserved in the Sierra, King's Canyon, and Sequoia national forests. Another trip saw him go searching for glaciers in Nevada. Still another, made in 1879, took him to Alaska, where he became the first white man to visit the glacial area now known as Glacier Bay National Monument. Nearby, he found the immense glacier that was later named Muir Glacier in his honor.

On his return from Alaska, Muir and his Louie Wanda were married. They settled on her family's ranch. There they stayed for many years and there they raised their two daughters, Annie Wanda and Helen. The passing years saw Muir working harder than ever. He gave much of his time to the ranch and its fruit harvests. He wrote his nature articles. And for three to four months each year, he went into the field. The passing years saw him return to Alaska and visit such distant lands as India, Russia, and Australia.

During the 1880s, Muir began to write articles that were more than explanations of nature's wonders. For years, he had been worried about how the lumber industry was greedily cutting America's forests away to nothing. He was especially troubled about his beloved forests of the West. As early as 1876, he had begun to say that the U.S. government should set aside some forest lands as national parks and reserves. It was the only way to save countless trees so that they could be enjoyed by future generations. More and more, his articles of the 1880s took up this theme and started him on the way to becoming one of the greatest American conservationists of the day.

In 1889, Muir took another step. He launched a campaign to have Congress set aside two California areas as national parks. Working with him was his good friend Robert U. Johnson, the editor of a magazine that published much of Muir's work. The campaign succeeded. In 1890, Congress established Yosemite National Park and, to the south, Sequoia National Park with its magnificent redwood trees. Muir was especially delighted by the formation of the Yosemite park. It covered 1,189 square miles and spread through the lands all about his beloved Yosemite valley. The valley itself was a state park at the time. It later became a part of the national park.

But Muir's work for conservation was not yet done. In 1896, he spoke with President Grover Cleveland on how the lumber companies were continuing to ruin the nation's forests. Cleveland wanted to save as many of the forests as possible. He had Muir help a group of nationally known conservationists write a report on what should be done. When completed, the report advised that two new national parks be formed (the Grand Canyon and Mount Rainier parks) and that the nation set aside thirteen new forest reserves. The reserves were to be located in eight western states. They were to cover 21 million acres.

President Cleveland had just a few weeks left in office and so did not have time to found the two parks. But he quickly issued an order that established the thirteen reserves. Instantly, the lumber companies took angry action. They had their supporters in Congress write a bill to cancel the order. On the opposite side of the fence, Muir and such conservation groups as the nationally known Sierra Club jumped into the battle. Muir sent letters to Congress and wrote magazine articles on behalf of the reserves.

Muir's articles did much to turn public opinion in favor of conservation. In 1898, the U.S. Senate voted for the bill to abolish the reserves. But the House of Representatives paid attention to public opinion and defeated the bill by a wide margin. The reserves were saved. The two national parks were formed later—Mount Rainier in 1899 and Grand Canyon in 1919.

It was a great triumph for Muir and the American conservation movement. Another triumph was his a few years later. In 1903, he and President Theo-

Overleaf: John Muir (left) and President Theodore Roosevelt as they rode out of Yosemite Valley during a camping trip in 1903.

dore Roosevelt went camping together in Yosemite valley. The President loved the outdoors and was an avid conservationist. He listened closely as Muir spoke of the great need to continue preserving the nation's forests. Muir's words had a great effect on the President, who launched a major conservation program during his term of office. Roosevelt added 250 million acres to America's national forests.

A LIFE CLOSES

John Muir was sixty-five years old and white-bearded when he and President Roosevelt went camping. He had eleven years left to live. They were to be busy and full years, though marred by the death of his beloved Louie Wanda in 1906.

He continued to write, concentrating now on a host of books. Among the books that flowed from his pen were *The Yosemite*, *The Mountains of California*, and *Our National Parks*.

He also went on traveling. During a 1906 trip, he discovered one of Arizona's petrified forests. The find, which he called the Blue Forest, contains fossilized wood 160 million years old. The Blue Forest was later added to the Petrified Forest National Park, which covers 147 square miles in eastern Arizona and contains the world's largest display of fossilized wood.

Two years later, 503 acres of giant coastal redwoods in northern California were set aside for the public's enjoyment by the U.S. government and named in his honor—the Muir Woods National Monument. The monument is located fifteen miles northwest of San Francisco.

In late 1914, Muir went to visit his daughter Helen at her home near Los Angeles. He fell ill with pneumonia and was rushed to a hospital. He died there on Christmas Eve at age seventy-six, leaving behind a treasure of services to his state and nation.

Left behind were writings that acquainted readers everywhere with the natural wonders of the West and the need to protect those wonders from commercial exploitation. Left was an increased understanding of how nature had created the magnificent Yosemite valley. And left were the national parks and forest reserves that he had helped bring into being. John Muir truly deserved the two titles that were bestowed on him by Americans everywhere—"Man of the Mountains" and "Father of Our National Parks."

CHAPTER SIX

Luther Burbank

LUTHER Burbank and John Muir were much alike. Both lived on farms as boys. Both gave their lives to nature. Both did their finest work in California.

But they differed in just as many ways. Muir traveled constantly. Luther Burbank settled in northern California and hardly ever strayed away. He spend fifty years there. All the while, he worked to create new varieties of fruits, vegetables, flowers, and grains. His creations won him lasting fame by improving the world's farm crops.

A SHY AND FRAIL BOY

Luther Burbank was born in a brick farmhouse near Lancaster, a small Massachusetts town, on

March 7, 1849. His father, Samuel, farmed the surrounding 100 acres and manufactured bricks from the clayey soil. Luther's mother, Olive, liked to spend hours working in her garden. He always thought that his love of nature came from her.

Samuel and Olive's son was shy as a boy. He was so shy that he seemed stupid when he went to school. He became tongue-tied and could not speak whenever he had to stand up and recite his lessons. His grades improved as soon as his teacher allowed him to write about what he was learning.

He was also frail as a boy. His frail health dogged Luther throughout his life. He was always thin. When he was in his teens, a section of the Burbank land caught fire. The blaze was caused by the sparks from a passing locomotive. Luther dashed through the summer heat for help. He fell ill with a severe sunstroke. Ever afterwards, he ran the risk of becoming weak or sick whenever he worked in the sun for long periods. For a man whose life's work kept him in the open, it was a heavy burden to bear.

But, in many ways, Luther was not shy and frail. He liked athletics and built all sorts of gymnasium equipment for his school. Ice skating was a favorite sport. One time, he made a small pool by damming a stream. He told everyone that he planned to study the insect life in the pool. What the boy really wanted was a skating rink when winter froze the spot over.

Sports were great fun, but Luther found his greatest joys in the woods and fields around his home. He was fascinated by all he saw—the plants and flowers, the trees, and the animals and insects. He soon became especially interested in the plants. He learned two lessons about them that were to lead him to his life's work.

TWO GREAT LESSONS

The first lesson began to take shape when Luther learned how plants reproduce themselves. They do so by taking in pollen from related plants. The pollen is carried to them by insects, the winds, and birds. The pollen enters a plant and unites with the female cells there. Together, they produce seeds for new plants.

But what was the lesson itself? It was that the pollen from a plant of one variety sometimes reaches a plant of another variety. When this happens, special seeds are created. They are special because they often produce plants that are stronger and better than the parent plants. This happens, however, only when the two varieties are related to each other in some way.

An exciting thought struck Luther when he learned about the special seeds. How interesting it would be to join different varieties of plants together and produce new and improved ones.

The second lesson came when Luther's uncle—Levi Sumner Burbank—paid a visit to the farm. Uncle Levi, who was a well-known scientiest in Boston, showed him how to cut a bud from an apple tree and graft it—carefully fasten it—to the seedling of a pear tree. In Luther's eyes, a miracle then occurred. The grafted bud took control and caused the pear seedling to grow into an apple tree. Uncle Levi explained that the same thing could be done with other trees and plants so long as they were closely related.

Luther was fourteen years old at the time. A new thought burst into his mind. Wouldn't it be wonderful to join different plants with the aim of producing new and better fruits and vegetables for people to eat—and new and more beautiful flowers for them to enjoy?

With this thought, Luther found his life's work. He would be a horticulturist, a worker with plants. But he would labor with them for the purpose of finding new food and greater beauty for the world.

THE FIRST SUCCESS

Luther attended school at Lancaster until his late teens, but did not go on to study at a university. Despite his frail health, these years were full and busy ones for him. He helped work the family farm. He earned money at various jobs. And he constantly experimented with the growing of plants in preparation for his life's work.

That work began in earnest in 1870. His father had just died and the family had sold their farm. A share of the money came to the twenty-one-year-old Luther. He used it to buy a small farm at the nearby town of Lunenburg. To support himself while he continued his experiments, he planted corn, vegetables, and potatoes. He planned to sell them at harvest time.

Luther Burbank always remembered the decision to grow potatoes as a lucky one. One of their number brought him his first success as a breeder of new plant varieties.

On a day in 1872, he came upon a strange sight as he was checking his potato crop. He glimpsed a plant with a green ball attached to it. On looking closely, Burbank saw that it was a seed pod. Potato seed pods were very unusual. They were hardly ever produced. And, whenever they did appear, they were thrown away. Every farmer knew that, unlike most other seeds, they did not produce good potatoes. Rather, they gave birth to oddly shaped and stunted potatoes that were never wanted as food.

And so, farmers always planted the potatoes themselves. They cut them into chunks that were then buried. Each chunk sprouted a plant that, when pulled from the earth, revealed a batch of young potatoes clinging to its roots.

But, as Burbank looked at the pod, he told himself that he would not throw it away. He remembered that the seeds of mingled plants can produce plants stronger and better than the parents. Perhaps there had been a mingling here. He would plant the seeds and find out. It might be that some of their number would not sprout poor and misshapen potatoes. Some might come up with a new and improved variety of potato.

The pod contained twenty-three seeds. Burbank

carefully planted and tended each one. At harvest time, he found exactly what he had hoped to find. Most of the plants had borne a poor crop. *But a few had come up with fine looking potatoes.* There was no doubt that they were a new variety that looked better and stronger than their parents. For the next two years, he cut these potatoes up and planted them. He was elated to see each planting bring forth even finer looking and tastier potatoes.

In 1875, Burbank took his latest and best crop to James Gregory, a merchant who sold seeds to the surrounding farms. He offered to sell Gregory all the rights to grow and sell the new variety of potato to farmers for planting. Gregory accepted and gave his visitor a check for a mere $150. It was one of the greatest bargains in the history of farming. Since then, the famous Burbank potato—or Idaho potato, as it is also called—has served as an excellent food for countless people.

CALIFORNIA AND 20,000 PRUNE TREES

Burbank did one thing with his new-found wealth. After selling his farm, he used it to buy a railroad ticket to California. He had always wanted to go there because the climate and soil were especially good for plant growth. He arrived in late 1875. A short time later, he was living on a two-acre plot in the midst of fine farming country.

His plot was located eighty-five miles north of San Francisco, at the town of Santa Rosa. Rather than becoming a farmer again, he opened a small plant nursery and began selling seeds and trees to the nearby farms. Conducting his plant experiments all the while, Burbank spent the next years earning a modest living at his nursery. Then, suddenly, his life changed.

In March, 1882, a wealthy merchant, Warren Dutton, came to see him. Dutton said he was launching a new business venture. He planned to grow the kind of plums that would not rot when left in the sun. Rather, they would dry out and become prunes. He was sure that the prunes would make him a fortune. Once dried, they would remain safe to eat for months to come. This meant that he could ship them to markets in the East.

But there was a problem. Everyone said that it took eighteen months or more to grow the plum trees needed for prunes. Dutton did not want to wait that long. He wanted to start his business as

Luther Burbank

soon as possible. He needed 20,000 young trees by
the coming autumn so that he could begin to harvest them next year. He had tried to order them
from every farmer in the area, only to hear that
they could not possibly be grown in such a short
time.

And so he had come to the Santa Rosa nursery.
He had heard of Burbank's experiments. He would
be willing to pay a good price for the trees if Burbank could pull off a miracle and have them ready
by the fall.

The horticulturist replied that he needed a little
time to think about the matter. That night, he re-
called Uncle Levi's long-ago lesson in plant grafting. He hit upon a plan that would enable him to
"pull off the miracle." The next day, he told Dutton
that the 20,000 young trees would be ready not by
fall but soon thereafter—in December. Dutton nod-
ded happily. December would be fine.

Burbank got down to work in a strange way.
After renting five acres for the project, he bought
and planted 20,000 *almond* nuts. As odd as the purchase seemed to be, it was all a part of his plan.
Burbank knew that the almonds would sprout into
tiny trees very quickly. He saw them take just three

months to do the job. Then it was time for the next step in his plan.

He went to a neighbor farmer who owned an orchard of the plum trees used for prunes. He purchased 20,000 buds from the trees and took them home to put Uncle Levi's lesson to use. He hired seventeen men to assist him and grafted the buds to the tiny almond trees. Burbank knew that the graftings would prove successful because the almond and the plum were closely related. Just as the apple bud had caused the pear seedling to grow into an apple tree long ago, the plum buds now took control. They turned the fast-growing almond seedlings into trees with plums that could be dried into prunes.

The result: Burbank filled most of Dutton's order in December. He delivered 19,500 young trees to the merchant. The remainder of the order was filled the next spring. In return for his work, Burbank received several thousand dollars.

His feat astonished all his neighbor farmers. They had thought him mad for taking on the Dutton job, but he had proved them wrong. Further, he had accomplished his miracle on a grand scale. The art of grafting had been used for centuries. But no one had ever tried to *mass produce* new plants with it. Now Burbank had tried it—and it had worked. It could now be used to increase the world's crop yields.

FULL AND BUSY YEARS

Burbank used a portion of the Dutton payment to buy four acres in what is now a busy area in the city of Santa Rosa. He first lived there in a white cottage. Later, he built a two-story home on the property. His mother and his sister Emma came west to keep house for him. His family increased by one when, at age forty-one, he married Helen Coleman. The marriage was not a happy one and ended in divorce within a few years.

The Dutton feat truly launched Burbank's career as a breeder of new plants. His four acres became the center of his life, along with eight acres that he purchased some miles away. Paying no attention to his frail health, he took on a schedule of work that would have broken many a stronger man. It was work that made him world-famous. It saw him develop more than 800 new varieties of fruits, veg-etables, flowers, grains, grasses, and food for livestock. In all, he produced what seemed to be an endless stream of miracles.

And what were these miracles? There were plums larger than had ever been seen before. There were tiny peas of a uniform size that made them easy for packers to can. There were peach trees that were able to bear fruit in cold climates where peaches had never before survived. There were new varieties of chestnuts, quinces, apples, and nectarines. There was a tasty walnut called the Royal. There were beautiful roses, lilies, and daisies. Of the flowers, Burbank's favorite was the brightly-colored Shasta daisy, which is now found throughout the state.

One of Burbank's finest accomplishments came in the 1880s when he heard that a red and sweet-tasting plum grew in Japan. At the time, American plums were small and black. They worked well in jams but were not eaten raw because they were so sour. Burbank imported twelve buds from the red plum's tree and grafted the best of their number to various American plum trees. The result: today's popular Satsuma plum.

A middle-aged Luther Burbank standing in the experimental gardens at his home in Santa Rosa.

Another major accomplishment grew out of a visit to the Southwest. On studying the cactus there, Burbank realized that it would make an excellent food for cattle that grazed on dry lands where there is little grass. That is, it would do well if only it was not covered with sharp spines. The result: three kinds of spineless cacti that have since served as fine animal fodder. This accomplishment, however, had a drawback. The cactus plants often grew spines if not eaten within a short time.

Burbank never worked on just one project at a time. He always had many different experiments all going at once. To get everything done, he hired a small army of assistants through the years. They all came to see him as a quiet-spoken and friendly man who was also a hard and patient scientist.

He was seen as hard because he believed in the theory held by the great British naturalist, Charles Darwin. Darwin said that new species take shape through a process called natural selection. This means that nature allows only the strongest of its members to survive and evolve. The weak die off and become extinct. Burbank not only believed the theory but also used it in his search for new plants. He wanted only the strongest and best varieties. And so, despite his love of all plants, he quickly threw away any that showed themselved to be weak and sickly. Countless such plants were cast aside over the years.

His assistants saw him as patient because he was willing to work for years to create a new and improved plant. His work in finding ten new types of berries gives a fine example of his patience. The quest lasted thirty-five years and involved experiments with over fifty different varieties of the *Rubus* berry.

The assistants also saw him as a very practical man. They found that he was never interested in growing new plants for the sake of gathering knowledge about them and nature. Rather, he wanted only to produce new food plants that would better feed the world, and new flowers that would bring it greater beauty.

THE LAST YEARS

From the day of his arrival, Burbank worked for just over fifty years at Santa Rosa. The last of those years were especially good ones for him. His many plant varieties were being welcomed everywhere and had made him wealthy and world-famous. He

was asked to give public lectures. The greatest figures of the day—among them inventor Thomas A.
Edison—paid him visits. And, when he was in his
sixties, he married again. His new wife was Eliza-
beth Waters. This time, the marriage was a happy
one. It lasted until his death.

A white-haired Burbank was working with roses
in the hope of creating blooms of a finer color when
the years of work came to an end. In late March,
1926, he suffered a heart attack. He seemed to get
better in the next days, but then fell more deeply
ill. Just after midnight on April 13, Luther Burbank
died at the age of seventy-seven.

To this day, the name of Luther Burbank remains
famous over the world. He is remembered not only
because he gave us more than 800 new and useful
plant varieties. Much of his fame rests on the fact
that his work helped turn the breeding of plants
into a modern science. In turn, the science has helped
yet another science—modern genetics, the study
of the mystery of how all life originates and de-
velops.

Further Reading

IF you would like to read more about the seven famous builders of California whose lives are sketched in this book, you need only visit your nearest library. You'll find a number of books about them on the shelves. Here are some that should prove especially helpful and interesting.

FATHER JUNIPERO SERRA

Wise, Winifred E. *Fray Junipero Serra and the California Conquest*
  New York: Charles Scribner's Sons, 1967
Bolton, Ivy. *Father Junipero Serra.*
  New York: Julian Messner, 1966
Demarest, Donald. *The First Californian: The Story of Fray Junipero Serra*
  New York: Hawthorn Books, 1963

Hawthorne, Hildegarde. *California Missions: Their Romance and Beauty.*
New York: D. Appleton-Century, 1942

JOHN C. FRÉMONT

Burt, Olive. *John Charles Frémont: Trail Marker of the Old West.*
New York: Julian Messner, 1955
Carlson, Vada F. *John Charles Frémont: Adventurer in the Wilderness.*
New York: Harvey House, 1973

JOHN SUTTER

Zollinger, J. Peter. *John Sutter: The Man and His Empire*
Gloucester, Massachusetts: Peter Smith, 1967
Dillon, Richard. *Fool's Gold: The Decline and Fall of Captain John Sutter of California.*
New York: Coward, McCann, 1971
Danna, Julian. *Sutter of California.*
New York: Press of the Pioneers, 1934

HENRY WELLS AND WILLIAM G. FARGO

Moody, Ralph. *Wells Fargo.*
New York: Houghton Mifflin, 1961
Loomis, Noel M. *Wells Fargo: An Illustrated History.*
New York: Clarkson N. Potter, 1968

Beck, Franklin M. *The Romance of American Transportation*.
New York: Thomas Y. Crowell, 1962

JOHN MUIR

Silverberg, Robert. *John Muir: Prophet Among the Glaciers*.
New York: G. P. Putnam's Sons, 1972
Swift, Hildegarde Hoyt. *From the Eagle's Wing: A Biography of John Muir*.
New York: William Morrow, 1963
Douglas, William O. *Muir of the Mountains*.
Boston: Houghton Mifflin, 1961

LUTHER BURBANK

Beaty, John Y. *Luther Burbank: Plant Magician*.
New York: Julian Messner, 1943
Dreyer, Peter. *A Gardener Touched with Genius: The Life of Luther Burbank*.
New York: Coward, McCann & Geoghegan, 1975
Kraft, Ken and Pat. *Luther Burbank: The Wizard and the Man*.
New York: Meredith Press, 1967

INDEX

Edward F. Dolan, Jr., is the author of more than sixty books for young people and adults. He worked for many years as a newspaperman and magazine editor, and has written numerous magazine articles and short stories.

A number of his books for teenagers have been histories of exploration and biographies. His *Adolf Hitler: A Portrait in Tyranny* was an ALA Best Book for Young Adults. He has also written on sports subjects and about mysteries of the air, of the sea, and of ice and snow.

Mr. Dolan is a native of California. He and his wife, Rose, live just north of San Francisco. They have two children, both grown and married.